GINGER GREEN

IS ABSOLUTELY MAD FOR Birthdays! (mostly)

Ginger Green is Absolutely Mad for Birthdays! (Mostly)
published in 2018 by
Hardie Grant Egmont
Ground Floor, Building 1, 658 Church Street
Richmond, Victoria 3121, Australia
www.hardiegrantegmont.com

A catalogue record for this
book is available from the
National Library of Australia

Text copyright © 2018 Kimberley Kane
Illustrations copyright © 2018 Jon Davis
Series design copyright © 2018 Hardie Grant Egmont

Design by Stephanie Spartels
Internals typesetting by Kristy Lund-White

Printed in Australia by McPherson's Printing Group,
Maryborough, Victoria, an accredited ISO AS/NZS 14001
Environmental Management System printer.

1 3 5 7 9 10 8 6 4 2

MIX
Paper from
responsible sources
FSC® C001695

The paper in this book is FSC® certified.
FSC® promotes environmentally responsible,
socially beneficial and economically viable
management of the world's forests.

GINGER GREEN

IS ABSOLUTELY MAD FOR Birthdays! (mostly)

hardie grant EGMONT

BY KIM KANE & JON DAVIS

For Lisa and Nell
(who was the very first reader)
and for Kelso, Toby and John.

– Kim

For Laura and Greta.

– Jon

CHAPTER 1

'My name is **GINGER!** Ginger Green.'

I am eight years old.

When I was in grade two, I was **really** into play dates. Now I am in grade three, I am still into play dates but I am also into **bigger kid things.**

I am allowed to stay up until quarter to eight.

I can sometimes sit in the front seat of the car.

POST
BOX

I can walk to the post box
all by myself, and ...

I am allowed to have
a **BIG** birthday party.

hooray!

'That's right!'

Today is Saturday. Today is my

BIRTHDAY.

Today is my **PARTY** too.
And I am mad for parties.

Two weeks ago, Mum said, 'Ginger Green,

you are turning eight. Eight is very grown-up.

Would you like to invite some friends to

come over for a party?'

'YES
PLEASE!'

So, I decided to have a

PRINCESS PARTY.

I decided on a princess party because ♥

I LOVE **beautiful things**.

♥ ♥

I love **drama** ➡

and **rock**

climbing.

I love

gymnastics

and **games.**

I love pretend and

MixMatch

dolls but I also love

princesses.

Princesses that are **sparkly** and **beautiful** and **very, very powerful** and go out and **slay dragons** and don't just sit around all day waiting for princes. We won't have any princes at the party.

Just princesses.

roar!

SO, my friend Lottie and I sat down to work out my party.

We wrote a list of all the girls I wanted to invite.

We wrote the invitations in

golden pen.

YOU'RE INVITED TO

Ginger Green's

PRINCESS BIRTHDAY PARTY

perfect

We sprinkled **sequins** and **glitter** inside. We sent out my invitations. We put them in the letterbox in a big envelope with a stamp. Each envelope had a **golden crown sticker** on the back like they might just be an invitation to tea from the Queen. We are not actually allowed to hand out

can't wait
can't wait
can't wait

invitations at school because it might hurt people's feelings. But posting invitations is

MUCH MORE FUN.

A proper princess party should have proper princess invitations. It makes your friends **VERY** excited.

After Lottie and I worked on my party list, I invited:

☆ **Lottie.** Of course. Lottie is in 3C this year and is possibly my very best friend of all.

☆ **Skye,** who is shy, from ballet.

☆ **Daya** who is tiny but definitely not cute, and very, very loud.

☆ **Meagan,** who is a bit annoying but very smart.

☆ **Maya,** who is an only child **BUT** likes my big sister Violet as much as me.

☆ **Zara and Georgie** who are twins and look identical on the outside, but are completely different on the inside. Like a peppermint choc-top and a strawberry choc-top.

✩ **Isla** who is my fanciest friend.

✩ **And Maisy,** who is my crazy friend. Actually, I was not going to invite Maisy because sometimes she can be a **BIT MUCH**. But she makes Lottie laugh. Lottie said if Maisy comes, she will keep an eye on her.

Not only did Lottie and I do the invitations to my party, we also designed my castle cake.

We designed my castle cake **ourselves** (with **some** help from my dad).

lollies!

We wrote a list of all the **party games** we would like to play. On the list we wrote:

☆ Pin the Ponytail on the Princess.

☆ The Chocolate Game.

☆ Make Princess Slime for craft.

☆ Musical Chairs.

Lottie is my best
friend AND my best
party planner.

Lottie came over
after school yesterday.

We set the party table.

We filled the party bags.

Each guest got
   a book of fairytales,
      a lolly ring,
         a real gem and
            a poison apple.

(The apple is not really poison. It is just
a red gummy lolly that I am calling a
poison apple for drama. I like drama.)

This morning
I woke up
very
early.

The party bags are lined up

on the kitchen bench.

I put on my **flouncy new**
princess dress.

My princess dress is
very fancy. It has a
great big sash
and it

twirls.

I pull on my crown.

Lottie and I made our crowns yesterday. We just couldn't wait. Our crowns are actually more like tiaras but they are very regal. I clipped mine on with hairpins.

Lottie is coming early. Lottie is coming at **nine-thirty** and the party starts one hour later. Lottie is coming to wait until the party starts in case I get nervous. (Getting nervous before a party is very normal.) Lottie will tie my sash if it comes undone and make sure my crown is not crooked. That's what a best friend and a best party planner do.

After breakfast, the phone rings. I am spinning around the kitchen in my new golden shoes and my new fancy dress.

My dress does **perfect** twirls.

whee!

Penny spins with me.

Penny is in clothes.

If you know my family, you know that is unusual. Penny is my little sister and she is **ALWAYS** nude. But today, Penny promised that she would wear a party dress too because it is a special day.

We spin **arooooouuuund** together. Mum answers the phone. She starts out with her happy high voice. Then her voice drops.

'Oh,' she says. 'Oh, that is a shame. Oh, poor Lottie.'

I stop spinning.

'A forty-degree fever? Oh, you must take her to the doctor,' Mum says into the phone. 'No, Ginger is fine. Perfectly healthy. Send Lottie our love. We will save a party bag for her. What rotten luck.'

SEND LOTTIE OUR LOVE?

what?

wait?

no!

oh!

'Lottie's sick?'

I look at Mum.

Mum nods.

I sit down. My best friend from 3C is sick? My best friend and party planner is sick?

I woke up full of joy and now I am full of despair. **Everything is going wrong.**

I cannot have a party without Lottie. Who will tie my sash if it comes undone? Who will straighten my crown if it is crooked?

And then something even worse occurs to me. I look at Mum. If Lottie is sick ...

WHO WILL KEEP AN EYE ON CRAZY MAISY?

oh no!

CHAPTER 2

Mum gives me a hug.

'It is definitely bad luck,' she says.
'Poor Lottie. Imagine how sad she must feel.'

I was feeling sorry for myself.
I was feeling so sorry
for myself, I hadn't
thought to feel sorry
for Lottie.

poor Lottie!

Now I feel even **worse**.

'Why don't we invite Edgar, from next door?' Mum asks. 'We have a spare spot without Lottie and I was feeling bad that we left him out.'

'OK,' I say.

I feel too sad

to say that Edgar only likes boy stuff, so I doubt he will want to come to a princess party.

I feel too sad to say it is actually a princess party with **no princes**.

I feel too sad for a party at all.

An hour later, I am feeling better. My big sister **Violet** helped me set up the chairs outside for musical chairs. She also did up my sash when it came undone.

Mum straightened my crown when it was crooked. Mum put special **sparkles** on my cheeks.

We hung balloons on the letterbox and on the front door.

I wait in the hall for my guests to arrive. I stare at my new shoes. I stare and spin. It is hard not to feel excited with new **gold shoes** and a **spinny dress** even though my best friend and party planner is sick. I wait for the doorbell to ring.

At ten-thirty, the doorbell does not ring. But there is a **thump** on the door.

THUMP! THUMP!

'Is that the door?' asks Dad. 'Maybe the bell is broken. Can you check please, Ginger? It might be your first guest!'

I run to the door.
I peek through the
spy hole. I see a bit
of a party balloon.
I see a sneaker.

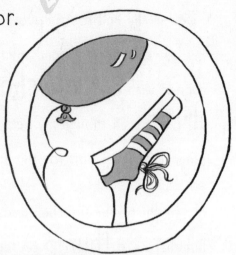

THUMP!

'Maisy?' I ask.

I open the door and Maisy falls down in front of
me - right down into a backbend.

'Hi Ginger,'

she says through her hands.

'Hi Maisy,' I say. 'You are not just my crazy friend, you are bendy as well.'

Oh dear. The last time I played with a bendy friend it ended in a **PLASTER CAST!** Maisy **FLIPS** her legs up into a handstand and ...

WALKS INTO OUR HOUSE ON HER *HANDS!*

'These days, I am mad for gym,' says Maisy.

She stands up. She is wearing jeans and sneakers.

GRUBBY jeans and **GRUBBY** sneakers.

Her face is red. 'And I am also mad for parties!'

'I am Ginger Green, Party Queen,'

I say. Seeing Maisy makes me miss Lottie

all over again. But I pat my birthday crown

and smile anyway.

'I am
MAD
for parties too!'

'Nice crown,' says Maisy.

'Thanks,' I say. 'You can make one later if you like!
We have crowns at the party table.'

A crown might jazz up your sneakers,
    I think. In grubby jeans and grubby sneakers,
Maisy is a very casual princess.

The doorbell
    rings.

RING
    RING!

who is it?

29

I turn around.

All my other friends have
arrived in a **big group**.

I see
Georgie
↓

...and
Zara.
↓

I see
Meagan,
↓

I see Isla,

Daya

and & Maya.

Isla passes me a very
fancy-looking present
with a great big
golden bow.

'Happy
birthday,
Ginger,' she says.
'Lovely dress!'

'Thank you, Isla,' I say. I am glad Isla
has noticed my fancy new dress.

Isla knows
fancy!

Edgar comes in next.

'You came in the front door!' I say. I am used to Edgar coming in over the fence.

'Yes,' he says. 'It seemed like the sort of thing to do at a party.'

Edgar looks at Isla and her big fancy present. He looks at Daya, Georgie and Zara, Meagan and Maya. 'Boy oh boy,' he says. 'You have LOTS of girls at this party.'

'Yes, but **ALL TYPES** of girls,' says Maisy, who is upside-down again. She waves a sneaker at Edgar.

'That is clever,' says Edgar.

'Is it?' asks Meagan. Meagan looks disapproving. Meagan does not go to many parties. Meagan does not go to many parties where the guests are

UPSIDE DOWN!

'That looks like fun,'

says a man's voice.

I look up.

'**HAPPY BIRTHDAY, GINGER!**'

says Skye's dad.

shy!

'Thank you!' I say.

I see a little peep of skirt.

I put my head around the door. 'Hi Skye!'

I take Skye's hand and pull her inside.
She looks very **NERVOUS**.

'You know Daya from **ballet** too,' I say.

Daya takes Skye's hand.

Daya comes up to Skye's elbow. Even Skye cannot be scared of Daya. Skye and Daya smile.

'**Bye**,' I say brightly to Skye's dad. 'See you later,' I add so he knows it is time to leave. I am excited about my party but it would be a very different party with Skye's dad there.

HE MIGHT DANCE.

'Have a good time!'
Skye's dad says, and winks.

'We will,' I reply.

And the thing is, I think we will. I feel **VERY** excited now. I don't even mind that Maisy is in grubby sneakers and Lottie **isn't** here at all. Mum says my only job at the party is to make sure my friends have a good time.

When all my friends are together, how can they **NOT** have a good time?

CHAPTER 3

We all walk into the dining room. Everybody **SQUEALS** when they see the table. There is a lovely **stripey tablecloth** and **pretty cups** and **special napkins**. There are also special straws. The straws have tiny crowns and ribbons for our

ROYAL FEAST.

There are pens and sequins and jewels and glue
my friends can use to decorate paper crowns
just like mine.

There is party food, too. There are **chips** and
cut-up carrots. We all know nobody
will eat the carrots but it makes Mum feel better.
In the middle of the table is a **big golden stand**
to put the cake on later.

The cake Lottie and I designed is in the pantry. It is a castle cake for a **party princess** just like we planned.

There are two rolling hills in golden buttercream.

There is a little castle on the top made from **lollies** and *ice-cream cones* and **sugar crystals**.

There will be eight **golden** candles.

It is BEAUTIFUL. It is the most

beautiful castle cake I have ever seen. It took Mum

and me three whole days to make it.

'Games **first**, party
food **second**,' says Mum.

My friends
look at the
carrots.

Nobody
complains.

'FIRST GAME, MUSICAL CHAIRS!'

I call.

We all go into the back garden.

Violet sits down at the laptop. She starts the music.

Everybody walks **round and round**

the chairs. Everybody except Maya.

Maya sits on the side next to Violet.

Violet lets Maya push pause on the laptop.

Maya looks very happy that Violet is letting her help. Maya looks very happy pushing pause like a grown-up.

At first I am a bit hurt as Maya is my friend. Maya is my friend and it is **MY PARTY**, <u>**not**</u> Violet's party. But then I remember that my only job is to **make sure my friends have fun**. Maya does not have any siblings, so she doesn't usually get to play with sisters. I am sort of happy Maya is having a good time.

I guess?

Maya won't join in, but Daya **CAN'T** join in.

SHE IS TOO SHORT!

When the music stops, Daya is just too short to jump up on the chairs.

pipsqueak

Daya is still trying to get on a chair when Maya starts the music. Then it stops again right away.

Skye has a seat,

but she helps lift **Daya** up onto another chair.

While Skye is

helping Daya, Maisy **steals** Skye's chair.

Rude!

Skye looks SHOCKED.

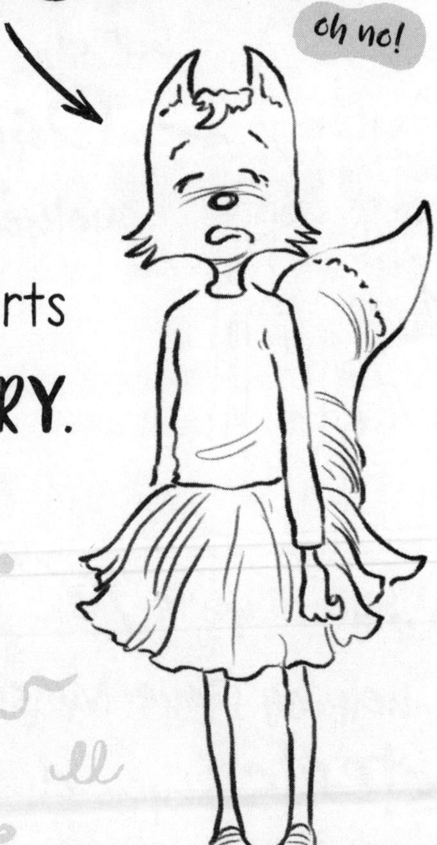

Skye starts to **CRY**.

'**MAISY!**' I call.

'Maisy, **THAT WAS NOT KIND!**'

'Sorry,' calls Maisy.

She springs off the chair into a handstand. Maisy is mad for walking on her hands now.

Penny is watching Maisy.

Penny LOVES Maisy.

Penny does a → handstand too.

She falls down.

whoops!

Penny does **ANOTHER** → handstand.

She stays up. But her dress falls ...

DOWN

DOWN

DOWN

... and over her head.

'Pants on, Penny,' says Violet in a whisper.

'But she's not nude,' I say to Violet. 'She is wearing a dress. It spins.'

I look over. Penny is wearing a dress. But she has forgotten her knickers.

Penny's **BARE BOTTOM** is right there in the air.

uh-oh!

49

'Penny!' I shout.

Maisy looks over at Penny. Maisy starts to laugh. Maisy falls over, and ...

⇒ SMASHES ⇐
INTO MEAGAN.

Meagan's glasses get knocked off her face.

Meagan tries to find them.

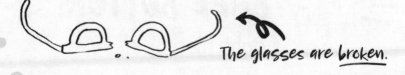

The glasses are broken.

'My mother is going to kill me,' says Meagan.

'**Without my glasses** I cannot read.

Without my glasses I cannot practise the violin.

Without my glasses –'

Meagan is now shouting.

'Wear mine,'

says Maisy.

Maisy hands

Meagan her glasses. 'They always slip off when

I am upside-down anyway.'

'Your glasses might be right for YOUR eyes,

but they will not be right for MY eyes,' says

Meagan. She gives Maisy and her glasses a

VERY NASTY LOOK.

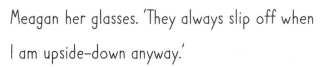

Mum takes Meagan to the study to **sticky-tape** her glasses back together.

Dad takes Penny to her bedroom to **put on some pants.**

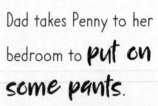

Pants on, Penny!

My party is **NOT** going well. My only job is to make sure my guests are having fun. But Daya **CAN'T** get on a chair. Maya **WON'T** get on a chair. Skye is **crying** because of Maisy. Maisy has **smashed** Meagan's glasses. Meagan can't see. And Lottie isn't even here.

'How much longer?' I ask Violet.

Violet looks at her watch. 'This party has been going for **five minutes**,' she says.

'FIVE MINUTES?'

I say.

'Six at most,' says Violet.

Five minutes and **I am NOT having fun.** Five minutes and my party has barely started. Five minutes and we have already finished one game! Five minutes and NOBODY is having a good time at all.

CHAPTER 4

'Let's play **Pin the Ponytail on the Princess!'** I say.

Pin the Ponytail on the Princess was Lottie's idea. I have drawn the princess. I have drawn the princess and made a long ponytail to pin on her her **royal head**.

'**NO WAY.**'

says Edgar.

'Why not?'

I ask.

'I will play some games, but I am not playing a princess game,' says Edgar.

'Ponytails and princesses are **NOT FOR BOYS.**'

'Or girls,' say Georgie and Zara.

'We're not mad on princesses.'

'Me neither,' says Maisy.

'Boys can have ponytails,' I say,

ignoring the twins and Maisy.

'That's true,' says Edgar.

'Boys can have buns, too,' I say. 'Boy buns.'

'That's true, too,' says Edgar.

Zara picks up the ponytail pin.

Georgie screams.

Or maybe Georgie picks up the ponytail pin and Zara screams. It is so chaotic, I can't tell them apart.

'It's not pin the ponytail on your **sister**,' I say.

'Georgie would look **lovely** with a ponytail,' says Zara.

oh no!

'Whose idea was this game?' asks Dad, taking the ponytail from Zara.

'Why don't we make the slime now?'
I suggest. 'That has no princess ponytails and no pins.
We just have to make it.'

'That sounds safer,' says Dad. **'Great idea.'**

'**Great idea**,' says Edgar.

'**Great idea**,' say the twins.

Lottie and I **LOVE** making slime.
Lottie and I especially love glitter slime. We bought
glitter paint and special powder called borax to
make the slime. You just mix the paint and the borax
together with a bit of water and hey presto, slime!
It is like magic!

pssst! If you
like making slime too,
turn to page 112 for
my secret recipe!

Dad sets everything up at the kitchen table.

Each kid gets their own bowl and spoon.

Mum **carefully** pours a little bit of borax and hot water into each bowl. Then Dad asks every kid to choose a paint colour.

There is **pink glitter paint.** There is purple glitter paint and there is blue glitter paint. There is also extra gold glitter and sequins.

Edgar looks at the colours. I wait for Edgar to say,
*'I do not like pink and I do not like purple. Pink and
purple are **girls'** colours.'* That is what happens when
you invite a **BOY** to a princess party.
I should have known.

Instead, Edgar says,
'I'll have purple, please.'

I raise an eyebrow.

So does Zara. Or maybe it is Georgie.

'Why?' asks Maya. 'Pink and purple are **girls'** colours.'

'They didn't use to be,' says Meagan. 'In the olden
days, pink was for boys and blue was for girls.
Blue was calmer.'

Edgar ignores Meagan.

'Purple is a ROYAL colour.

All the kings and emperors wore purple.

Roman emperors wore purple and gold.

Purple glitter paint with extra golden glitter is VERY ROYAL indeed.'

'Good choice,' says Dad.

Georgie and Daya and Maya all choose **PINK**.

Slime can sting a bit so I always mix with a spoon first!

Meagan chooses BLUE.

'The blue is not quite **dark** enough,' says Meagan.

She squeezes in some dark purple glitter paint. **'That's better.'**

'That colour is **VIOLET**,' says Violet. 'I should do that to mine too!'

We all mix our slime, first with a spoon, then with our fingers. Slime feels fabulous on your fingers. **Silky** and **stretchy**. It sort of puffs up as you mix it. The slime climbs up our hands and then our arms. It is sticky.

Meagan's slime is now a dark, rich violet. 'If I take some of Maya's and some of Edgar's, I can do this,' says Meagan, stretching her slime between her fingers.

'Do what?' asks Edgar. 'You are not taking **ANY** of my royal slime.'

'Make galaxy slime. When the colours are mixed together,' says Meagan, 'it looks like a

galaxy.'

Maya hands Meagan a strip of
pink glitter slime. Maya trusts
anybody who wears glasses.

Meagan moulds the
three bits of slime
together and then
stretches them out. It really does look like the galaxy.
The glitter really does look like **stars**.

'That's clever,' says Edgar.
'I'll make some too.'

Maya and Edgar also make galaxy slime.

Isla joins in. →

Isla has added extra glitter to her slime. She has gold and silver glitter.

'You can never have enough glitter,' says Isla.

'I agree,' says Edgar. 'Very royal.'

Edgar and Maya add sequins to their slime.

The sequins look like planets.

So many sparkles!

At the other end of the table, Maisy is making pink slime. Maisy is right into slime. It is the first thing Maisy has done without any fuss. She is making it with Penny. Penny is back from her bedroom with her dress and pants on. At least I **HOPE** she has pants on.

Maisy and Penny are carefully squeezing the slime like dough.

Slime, glorious slime!

tee-hee!

'I love slime,' says Maisy.

'I love slime too,' says Penny.

Maisy sees the pot of **STRAWS** on the party table, the straws with the crowns and ribbons.

'Go and get two straws,' says Maisy.

Penny sneaks over to the party table.

sneak sneak

Penny reaches up and takes two straws. Penny brings them back to the slime.

Mum sees Penny, but pretends not to. She is too busy mixing pink slime for Daya, who cannot see up over the edge of the bowl. Penny and Maisy put the straws in Maisy's slime.

← **THEY BLOW**.

The slime blows

UP

UP

UP

and makes an

ENORMOUS

slime
bubble.

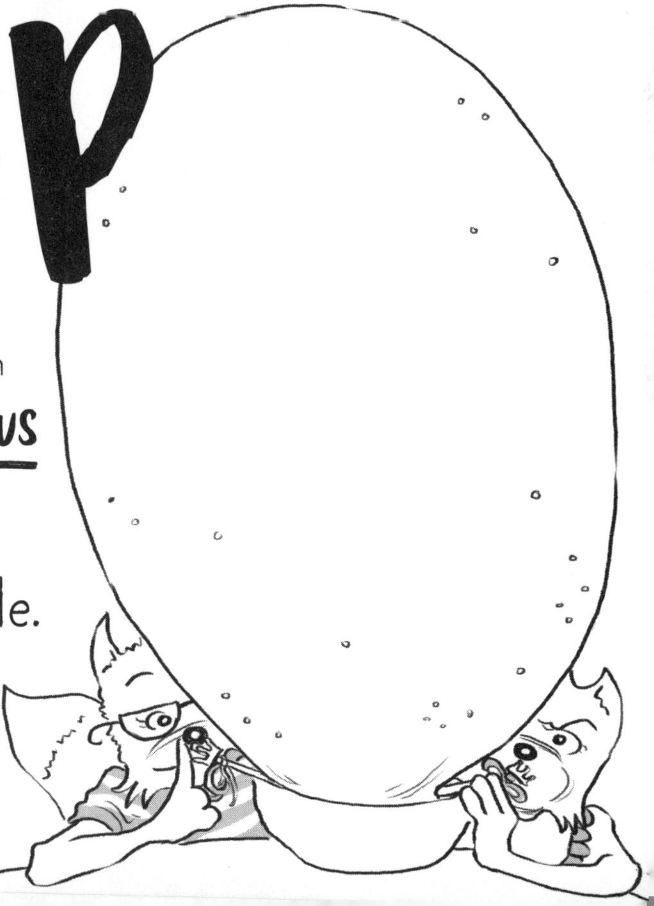

Maisy keeps blowing through
the straw up her nose.

Maisy blows.

The slime bubble gets bigger and
bigger. It sits fat and shiny in the
bowl like an enormous egg.

EVERYBODY **STOPS**
TO WATCH.

'I'll take those,' says Dad. 'The straws were for
the party table.' He reaches over. The bubble bursts.
The bubble bursts with a **BIG FART**. The bubble
bursts with a **BIG FART** and a **SQUELCH**.

SLIME FLIES
EVERYWHERE.

noooo!

Slime hits Meagan's glasses,
the ones Mum just sticky-taped.

Slime hits Isla in a great
blob all down the front
of her **fanciest**
party dress.

Slime flies over Daya's head
and snags Edgar's sneaker.

Slime flies **UP, UP, UP,**
and hits Dad right
... *in the face.*

not on Isla's
fancy dress!

Dad peels the pink glitter slime
from his face. He takes the pink
glitter slime from Edgar's shoe.

'OK, that's enough
slime for now,'

says Dad. 'You can take it home with

your party bags. Let's play the

CHOCOLATE GAME.

Outside.'

Dad **SOUNDS** fed up. Dad **LOOKS** fed up.

But it is hard to look fed up when you have

pink glitter slime in your eyebrows.

Mum quickly takes Isla and Meagan to the bathroom
to clean up Isla's dress and Meagan's glasses.

Dad takes everybody

outside for the

CHOCOLATE
GAME.

I am a bit
   relieved.

The chocolate game is my favourite game of all.

The chocolate game has **FIRM** rules.

It is hard to muck
up a game when
it has firm rules,
isn't it?

CHAPTER 5

I love the chocolate game.

It is an old-fashioned game. You need **dice**, **chocolate** and **dress-ups**.

Oh, and you need a knife and fork.

Firstly you have

to roll a dice.

If you get a **SIX**, you have to dress up.
I love dress-ups. Then you have to eat
chocolate with a knife and fork. I love chocolate,
even with a knife and fork. You get to eat as much as
you can until the next person rolls a six.

The chocolate game is a game of

CHANCE and a game of

SKILL.

It is the
PERFECT game.
Nothing can
go wrong!

First up,
Isla rolls
the dice. →

Then, **Georgie**
rolls the dice.

Then, **Zara**
rolls the dice.

Skye rolls the dice next.

'**SIX!**'
we all yell.

Skye puts on the **hat**.
She puts on the **gloves**
and the **scarf** and she
starts to cut the chocolate.
Skye is very good with
chocolate and a knife
and fork.

She eats slowly and she is not greedy.

She eats three pieces. Daya rolls the next **SIX**.

'**SIX!**'

Daya shouts.

Daya is tiny but still loud.

Skye takes off the dress-up clothes.

Daya throws them on.

Daya starts to eat.

Daya manages **three** pieces of chocolate before ...

Maisy throws a six.

Another six!

'SIX!'

Maisy is **EVEN LOUDER** than Daya, which is really saying something.

Maisy **does not bother** with the hat.
Maisy **does not bother** with the gloves.

Maisy **does not bother** with the scarf.
Maisy **does not bother** with the knife ...

or the fork.

Maisy just picks up the chocolate and
starts eating it.

what?!

'YOU CAN'T DO THAT,'

says Meagan.

'Rules are rules. You have to use your knife and fork.'

'You can't do that,' says Edgar. 'That's cheating.'

hey!

Maisy shoves **ANOTHER** row of chocolate in her mouth.

Daya ate three pieces of chocolate. Skye ate three pieces of chocolate. Maisy has eaten **FOUR ROWS**.

'Keep rolling the dice!' I say. 'Let's get her out.'

Maisy is no longer upside-down. Maisy is up and about.

Maisy is up and about and **FULL UP** of chocolate.

'**SIX!**' yells Georgie and pulls on the gloves. *finally!*

Maisy stands up and burps.

BUUUURRRPP!

'I am going to the kitchen,' she says.

Maisy really is <u>crazy!</u>

CHAPTER 6

When the chocolate is just about gone,
Mum comes outside. 'You are playing nicely now!

Don't speak too soon ...

Who's ready for some food?'

'ME!'
we all yell.

We walk to the **beautiful**
party table and sit down.

We start to make our **crowns**.

There are two **EMPTY** → chairs.

'Who is missing?' asks Mum. She looks around. **'Maisy,'** says Mum. 'Where is Maisy?'

'Where is Penny?' asks Dad.

Dad looks at Mum.

Mum looks outside. Mum looks out the window and up at the **garage roof**.

Last time Maisy came over, she ended up on the

garage roof in her undies.

But today, Maisy is **NOT** on our roof.

We learnt that Maisy loved climbing the hard way.

Today, Maisy is not in her **UNDIES** on our roof.

'MAISY IS NOT ON THE ROOF AT ALL.'

says Mum.

'Well, that's good news,' says Dad.

'Not **BAD** news is not **GOOD** news,' says Mum. 'We still don't know where Maisy and Penny are.'

'I'll find them,'

I say.

I go into the
BEDROOM.

Maisy and
Penny are
not in our
bedroom.

I go into the
PLAYROOM.

They are not in
our playroom.

I go into the **KITCHEN**.

They are not in the kitchen.

And then I hear a **WHISPER**.

I hear a

WHISPER

and a **GIGGLE**

from the pantry.

The pantry door is closed.

The pantry door is **NEVER** closed.

I open the door.

THERE IS MAISY.

THERE IS PENNY.

There is my **beautiful** castle cake.

Only my **beautiful castle cake** is not beautiful anymore. My beautiful castle cake does not have a castle. My beautiful castle cake is **NUDE**. My beautiful castle cake is just two golden buttercream hills.

My beautiful castle cake looks like A BOTTOM.

CHAPTER 7

I AM ANGRY.

I am angrier than I have **EVER** been.

'You <u>**RUINED**</u> musical chairs. You cheated in the chocolate game and now you have eaten the castle on my beautiful cake,' I say. I am crying.

Penny has **buttercream** on her fingers and her nose. Maisy has buttercream on her fingers and **UP** her nose.

'I feel a bit **SICK**,' says Maisy.

'I feel a bit sick too,' says Penny quietly.

They both know they have done something very wrong. They both know they have done something very, **VERY** wrong.

'It just looked so **beautiful**,' said Maisy.

'It **was** beautiful,' I say sadly. I am eight years old today. I wanted a castle cake for my party.

Instead I got a cake that looks like a BARE BUM.

'It is **MY** party,' I say to Penny.

'It is **MY** party,' I say to Maisy.

Maisy looks **SAD**. Penny starts to **CRY**.

'I was actually having fun,' says Maisy.

'You were having fun, but I didn't have fun. I don't think Meagan or Skye were having fun either. I am the **birthday girl** and I am not having a good time,' I say.

'I am sorry, Ginger,' says Maisy.

Maisy looks around. 'I am good at climbing. I am good at handstands, but I am not very good at parties. Luckily, I have an idea,' she says.

Maisy picks up a jar of Smarties from the pantry shelf. Maisy opens the jar. Maisy starts to put lines of Smarties on my bottom cake. Maisy slowly covers the bottom in Smarties.

I stop crying. I help.

'Is it undies?' I ask. I turn to Penny. 'Penny, you may not recognise these, but they are called "pants".'

'Not just pants,' says Maisy. 'Smarty pants.'

We all laugh.

I stick the eight golden candles on top of the cake.

I carry my cake out to the party table.

I hold my hands

VERY STEADILY

and try not to trip.

'I thought you had a
castle cake?' says Edgar.

'It's a **smarty-pants cake**,' I say.

'That is so much **COOLER** than a **castle cake**,'

says Edgar.

'That is the funniest cake I have ever seen.'

Edgar starts to laugh. Everyone joins in.

I start laughing too.

'HA[

BIRT[

PPY

HDAY!

everybody sings.

I BLOW OUT THE CANDLES.

I cut the first slice of cake and put it on a plate.

'Give it to me!' says Daya.

'Give it to me!' says Edgar.

'Give it to me!' says Meagan.

Maisy and Penny don't say anything.

I wrap the cake in a
napkin. 'The first piece
is for Lottie,' I say.

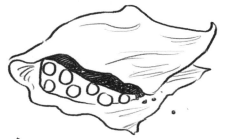

Everybody claps. Lottie designed
the castle cake with me. Lottie thought of the castle
and the rolling buttercream hills. Even so, Lottie
would find a bum cake very, very funny.

And very, very delicious.

I am
GINGER GREEN

and I am just a bit bigger.

Today, I had my eighth birthday party.

My eighth birthday party did not quite go

to plan but in the end I did have fun, even

though my best friend was sick. My other

friends had fun too. We all got to play games.

We all got lolly bags and we all ate cake.

Except Maisy and Penny. Maisy and Penny did not

want any cake but that left all the more for us.

A good time
was had by all.

THE END

HOW TO PLAN YOUR OWN
Princess Party

HOW TO MAKE
Glitter Slime

You don't need to COOK slime, but it is messy and the borax can ⇒ **STING** ⇐, so it's **probably best** to do this with a mum, a dad, a carer or a big sister or a big brother (as long as they have pants on).

YOU'LL NEED:

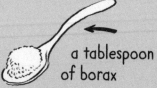

a tablespoon of borax

1 cup of glitter paint
(a 250 ml bottle is easily enough)

15 ml of HOT water →
(25 ml if you want to make your slime really gooey)

STEP 1

Mix borax and
water in a bowl
until almost dissolved. Add in the glitter paint.
You can use your hands but I start with a spoon.
Mum likes to wear rubber gloves but I like the way
the slime feels.

STEP 2

Knead the slime between your fingers,
mixing the glitter paint and the borax
mixture completely together. Sometimes the
slime can be a bit stringy to start with.

STEP 3

Leave the slime to sit for 5 minutes.

STEP 4 Squish and knead the slime again. It should feel like **real goo!**

STEP 5

Add extra glitter if you like it **super sparkly**.

STEP 6

If you make different colours you can mix them lightly together to make **rainbow** slime. I like purple, blue and pink best as it really does look like a galaxy when you stretch it out.

STEP 7

Wash your hands straight afterwards.

TIP:

Store the slime in cling wrap. If it gets too slimy, unwrap it and leave it to air out for half an hour.

MAISY'S TIP:

Stretch the slime out and put it in a bowl. Put a straw in the middle of the slime and **BLOW!**

DECORATE YOUR OWN
paper
crown

This is the perfect way to get guests to SIT DOWN when they are supposed to sit down at the table.

STEP 1 Photocopy page 118–119 onto thick yellow paper. You could even use golden paper. You will need one crown for every party guest, plus a few extra in case you have a sister like my little sister Penny or a friend like my friend Maisy.

You never know WHAT could happen to a crown with kids like that around!

STEP 2 Cut out all the crowns.

STEP 3 Put the crowns on the party table along with whatever you want to use to decorate them. We had **glue sticks** and **glitter** and **sequins** and **stick-on jewels**, but you might also like to use fancy buttons or stickers or shiny textas or whatever else you have around the house that the grown-ups won't **FREAK OUT** about.

'Penny, did you glue Grandma's **REAL** pearls on that crown?'

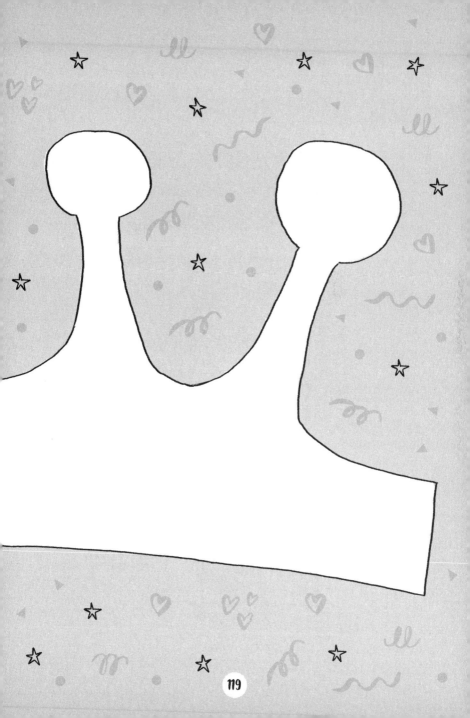

STEP 4 Once your guests sit down, ask them to decorate their crowns. When everyone is finished and the glue is dry, ask everyone to wear their **masterpieces**. We pinned ours on with bobby pins to help hold them in place. If we had time (and, if for example, Penny and Maisy had **NOT** turned my cake into a **BUM**), we would have had a

"MOST ROYAL CROWN"

competition.

If your castle cake with rolling buttercream hills is not turned into a **BARE BOTTOM**, you might like to have your own royal competition!

Some of your friends,
    maybe kids like Edgar, might
like to decorate other ———→

    shapes instead.

WELL, TOUGH.

This is a crown competition. If they don't want to join in, send them to the slime table instead.

Or tell them
    you'll cut off
    their head.

BY ROYAL
DECREE

HOW TO USE
mini
crowns
TO MAKE YOUR PARTY LOOK **EXTRA** FANCY

Photocopy the mini crowns on page 124–125 onto
yellow or golden paper, or even silver if you like
silver better than gold but honestly, **WHO DOES?**
Cut the crowns out and use them as party decorations.

We used gold ones. We wrote the guest's names on the crowns in Lottie's very **best handwriting** and then stuck them onto the lolly bags. We used glitter glue and glitter gel pens! Mine sure was **one royal party**.

We also stuck the crowns to the top of a straw with sticky-tape. We tied purple and gold ribbons underneath the crown so it looked like a royal wand, which is called a **sceptre**. You could make one of these for every guest or you could make just one and use it as a prize for a party game.

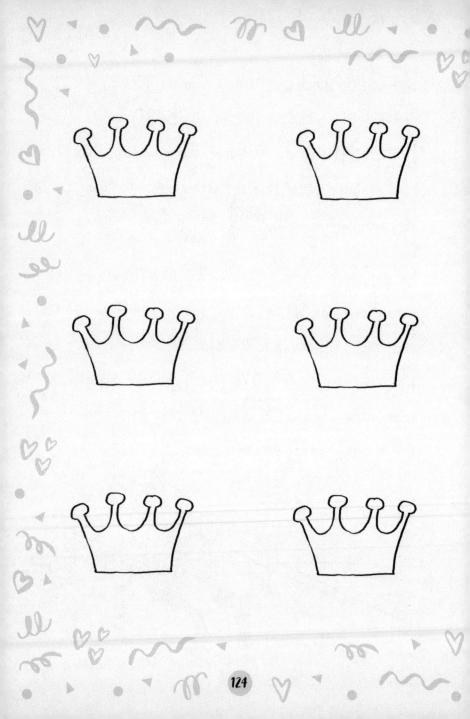

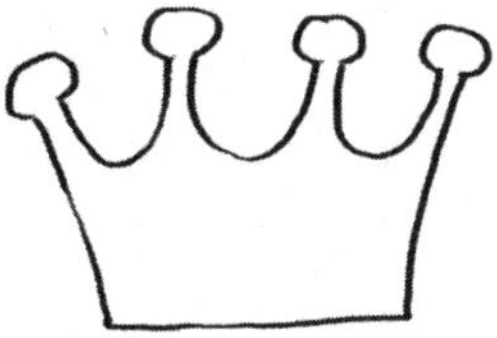
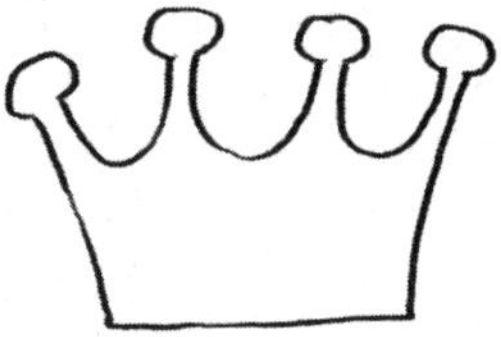
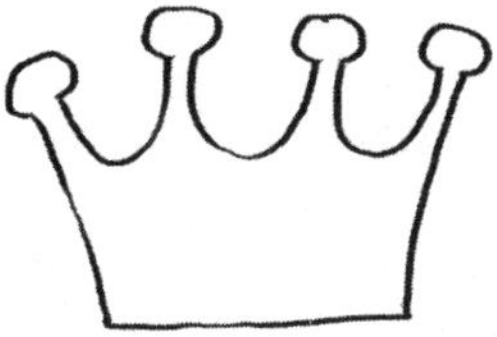
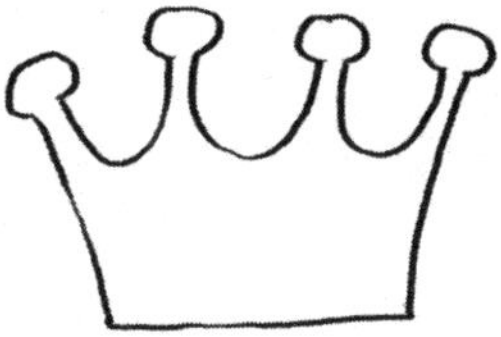
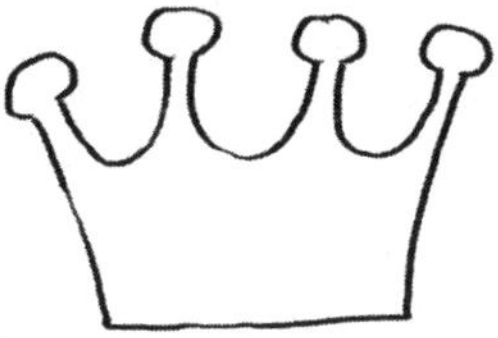
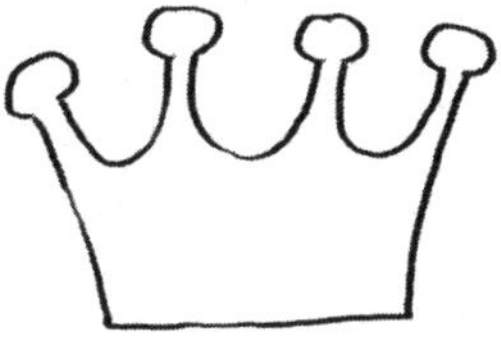

Apart from crowns and a scepter, queens and kings can also have **orbs**, which are big golden balls. If you are mad for ball games like Edgar, you could have a basket of golden balls on the table, like the ones you use for handball. You could even play a ball game with them later on.

Because Lottie and I are **NOT** mad for ball games and in fact **can't stand**  them, we didn't have orbs, but if you want some and you don't have any golden balls handy then you could use something else, like golden balloons or even ping pong balls coloured with gold texta. If that sounds too tricky, you could use yellow lollies or round chocolates that have gold wrappers instead.

See what you can find!

THE royal dash

This is a game that Lottie and I planned, but we didn't end up playing it. If you don't have a guest like Maisy then **you** could play this one! I might even play it on the weekend even though it is not my party anymore at all.

For this game you will need one pair of pantyhose or tights for each guest. The pantyhose or tights should be white or beige and very see-through and very stretchy.

The tights are going to represent

CROWNS.

Real crowns do not actually look like tights but honestly who is going to care?!

Blow up lots of balloons. I used jewel

colours like purple and emerald and ruby red as the

balloons will be jewels. Don't blow them up all the

way or you won't get enough jewels in your crown –

about halfway is good.

Each guest gets a pair of tights. When the grown-up in charge says **'Go,'** the guests have to **stuff their tights with the balloon-jewels.** When their crowns are full of balloon-jewels they have to put the tights on their head, just like a crown with very long spikes, and run to the other end of the garden (or the other end of the room if you don't have a garden).

The winner is the person who gets the crown to the other end of the garden **AND** has the most jewels in their crown.

If you want to make this game even harder, your guests could blow up their own balloons **before** stuffing them into their tights. Lottie and I did try it this way when we were planning the party games, but neither Lottie nor I are any good at tying balloons, so our crowns were just filled with sad saggy bits of rubber.

SCEPTRE AND ORB
Smash
AND Dash

If you are like Edgar and you like ball games, give each guest a yellow pool noodle. These will be used as pretend **sceptres**.

Blow up a golden balloon for each guest.

Each guest has to use their sceptre to hit their orb. The aim is to get from one end of the garden to the other **WITHOUT** letting your orb hit the ground.

The winner

is whoever gets to the end of the garden first with the **LEAST** number of ground-touches.

Well, you know how much I **HATE** ball games, but I honestly **LOVED** this one. If I had my party again I would do **Sceptre and Orb Smash and Dash** and forget all about **Pin the Ponytail on the Princess**. Edgar and Zara and Georgie would all be happier with that. If you get really sick of your guests, you could even smash and dash them instead.

Or chop off their heads.

That is the sort of thing a queen can do.

CROWN JEWEL
piñata

If your princess party is going to be in summer, you might like to try this. You should probably warn your royal guests that they might get wet during this game so they might like to change into their bathers before they play, even though you **NEVER EVER** see the Queen in bathers.

Fill jewel-coloured balloons with water. Don't use water-bomb balloons as they are too small for this game – use regular-sized ones. Tie the end of each balloon with string and attach them all to the clothesline.

Blindfold a guest and hand them a pool-noodle sceptre, or you could even hand them a plastic knight's sword. Kings and queens are also very partial to swords. We have a million in the toy box.

Blindfolded guests take the pool noodle or the sword and take it in turns to smash the water-filled jewels. You get one hit per turn.

The winner is the person who hits the last jewel down!

About the author and illustrator

KIM KANE is an award-winning Australian author who writes for children and teens. Her books include the CBCA short-listed picture book *Family Forest*, and her time-slip children's novel *When the Lyrebird Calls*. **Ginger Green** is the second series starring this funny and feisty fox. Ginger first appeared in *Ginger Green, Play Date Queen*, a beloved first-reader series.

Pirates, old elephants, witches in bloomers, bears on bikes, ugly cats, sweet kids – **JON DAVIS** does it all! Based in the Lake District, England, Jon has illustrated more than 60 kids' books for publishers across the globe, including *Ginger Green, Play Date Queen!*

Acknowledgements

I would like to thank the HGE team including Penny, Luna and Marisa, who could not be more tapped into our readership if they were eight themselves, and Hilary, with whom it all began. To Jon, Steph and Kristy for turning the words into illustrations and beautiful designs. I would like to thank my Australian agent Pippa, who fights contracts while raising a future readership. Finally, I would like to thank my early readers and aesthetic caucus who have provided such sage single-digit counsel including Amanda and Imogen, Michelle, Zara and Georgie, Tamsin, Peggy and Martha, Annabel, Amelia and Will, Mandy and Esau together with Nell and Lisa. Finally, I would like to acknowledge my children and their friends, whose quips and antics I shall shamelessly plunder for as long as they will let me. With love and thanks. – *Kim*

Thanks to Kim and the Hardie Grant Egmont chaps for giving me the chance to illustrate such fab books. – *Jon*

COLLECT them all!

THE NOT-MUCH Sleepover Starring GINGER GREEN

BY KIM KANE & JON DAVIS

Ginger Green is all about **friendship, FUN,** and **laughter** – even in the face of

⇒ DISASTER! ⇐

Ginger is going backyard camping with her **BFF** Lottie! She's excited about having a campfire, sleeping in a tent and even a **MIDNIGHT FEAST**. But what happens when their snuggly sleepover doesn't go to plan?